RONDA and DAVID ARMITAGE
ONE MOONLIT NIGHT

ANDRE DEUTSCH

To Jonathan

First published in 1983 by
André Deutsch Limited
105-106 Great Russell Street, London WC1B 3LJ
Second impression 1985
Third impression 1987
Fourth impression 1989

Phototypeset by Tradespools Limited, Frome, Somerset
Printed by Colorcraft Ltd., Hong Kong

ISBN 0 233 97540 3

First published in the United States of America 1983
Library of Congress Number 82-073994

STANDARD LOAN

UNLESS RECALLED BY ANOTHER READER
THIS ITEM MAY BE BORROWED FOR

FOUR WEEKS

To renew, telephone:
01243 816089 (Bishop Otter)
01243 812099 (Bognor Regis)

20.

When Tony was given a tent his dad got very excited.

"You'll have a marvellous time with this," he said, "the next fine weekend you can camp out all night."

Tony was horrified. "All by myself, all alone, all night?" he gulped.

"You needn't be alone if you don't like the idea," said Dad. "Ask Sam to join you."

Dad didn't have to wait long for a fine Saturday.

"It should be a perfect camping night," he announced, "cold and clear, lots of stars and a full moon." Tony and his friend Sam were not quite so sure.

"Right," said Dad, as he glanced at the tent plan, "we'll have this pitched in no time."

"Just pop up the poles, bang in a few tent pegs, tie the odd rope . . .

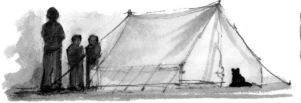

. . . and you've got a great
looking tent."
    He didn't notice the tent
collapse.

And the boys hadn't the heart to tell him.

It took most of the afternoon for Tony and Sam to move in.

"I brought my gumboots," explained Tony, "just in case it rains."

"I've brought something to drink," said Sam, "just in case we're thirsty, and I thought we might wake up early so I brought some toys."

"And I brought our largest torch," said Tony, "just in case . . ."

"Just in case," interrupted Lisa, "just in case you need to spot the Bogeyman."

Mum brought a delicious camping tea.
   "Just in case you're starving after moving house all afternoon,"
she laughed.

Night came slowly. The boys dressed in their warmest pyjamas, their woolliest socks and their warm dressing gowns.

"You'd better watch out for ghosts," said Lisa, "you can tell when they're about by the moaning and wailing."

"Don't be silly, Lisa," said Sam, "you don't get ghosts in gardens."

"Sleep well, boys," called Dad from the doorway, "I know you are going to have a great night – I wish I was coming with you."

Tony wished he was, too, but he kept this thought to himself.

It was quite dark by the time Tony and Sam had organized
themselves and their belongings in the tent. They snuggled down
into their sleeping bags and lay very still.

"It's very quiet when it's dark," whispered Tony.

"It's very dark when it's dark," whispered Sam, "even with a full
moon."

The boys lay still again. An owl hooted. "What's that?" squeaked
Sam.

"Don't be silly, Sam," said Tony, "it's just an old owl out
hunting. Go to sleep."

A cat yowled. "What's that?" squealed Tony.

"Don't be silly, Tony," said Sam, "it's only an old cat out fighting."

Something rustled near the corner of the tent.
   "What's that?" whispered both the boys together. But when they
listened again there wasn't a sound.

Inside was quiet too; Dad was busy reading the newspaper, Mum was busy yawning. Neither of them noticed that Lisa had disappeared.

The next noise outside was the sort of noise that sends shivers up
and down the spine.

"What was THAT?" gulped Tony, "it sounded just like a g-g-ghost."

"Don't be silly," said Sam, "I told you before you don't get ghosts in gardens."

"Perhaps this one's lost its way," whispered Sam. "Sssh, listen."

Again came the ghostly wail, but this time it was followed by a
not so ghostly giggle.

"Lisa," shouted the boys, "what a horrible thing to do. Go away and leave us alone."

"I heard you," said Lisa, shrieking with laughter, "you really thought I was a ghost, a ghastly, garden ghost." The boys could hear her laughing all the way to the kitchen door.

They tried to sleep again. "I'm cold now," grumbled Tony.

"So am I," said Sam, "do you know what I would like most of all right at this moment? I'd like a great, big, cup of steaming hot chocolate."

And before you could say Jack Robinson the boys were inside.

Tony and Sam took a long time to drink their chocolate.

"Did something frighten you out there, boys?" inquired Lisa. The boys glared at her.

"Lisa," said Mum crossly, "that's enough teasing for one night – bed for you."

"Dad," asked Tony, "just in case we wake up in the middle of the night, what would we do if we needed you?"

"Mmm," said Dad, "I hadn't thought of that." He scratched his head. "I know," he said, "I've got the very thing.

We start at
the tent like this . . .

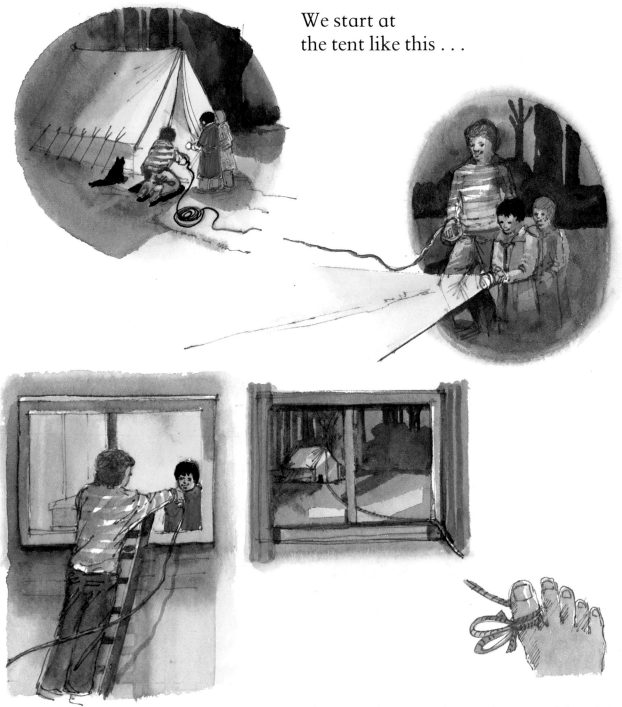

and we end up with my big toe like this.

If you need me just give the rope a tug and I'll come running.''

And everybody went happily to bed.

It was just after midnight when an owl, tired of hunting,
decided to rest.

"TWANG!" went the string on Dad's toe. Dad leapt out of bed,
untied the string and . . .

along the hall . . .

down the stairs . . .

out of the door . . .

and across the lawn he sprinted.

But when he peered into the tent the boys were sound asleep.

It was nearly 3 o'clock when the black cat sat down outside the tent to clean his whiskers.

"TWANG!" went the string on Dad's toe. Dad climbed wearily out of bed, untied the string and . . .

along the passage . . .

down the stairs . . .

out of the door . . .

and across the lawn he plodded.

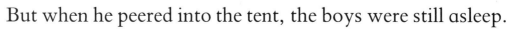

But when he peered into the tent, the boys were still asleep.

The early birds were beginning to whistle as the milkman made his way up the path.

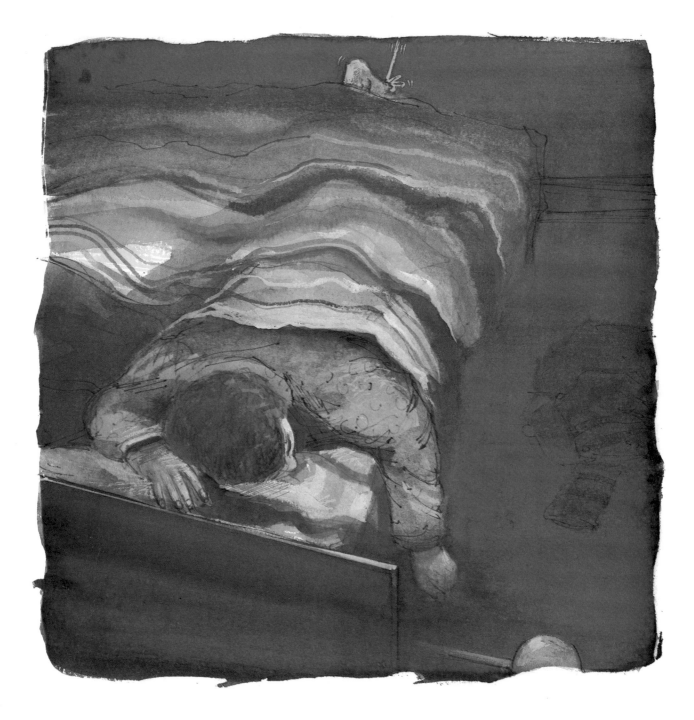

"TWANG!" went the string on Dad's toe. Dad crawled out of bed, untied the string and . . .

along the passage . . .

down the stairs . . .

out of the door . . .

and across the lawn he stumbled.

But when he peered into the tent the boys were gently snoring.

The boys were very pleased with themselves when they awoke.

"We did it," exclaimed Tony, "we slept all night and we didn't need to waken Dad once."

"I wonder if your father's string idea would really have worked," said Sam, "let's try it and see."

Tony tugged and waited. Nothing happened, nobody came running. He tugged again but still nothing happened. The boys were most indignant.

Tony's mother greeted them at the front door. "Don't disturb your father," she whispered, "he's hardly slept a wink all night."

And when they peered into the bedroom, there was Dad,
sound asleep.